MASK

DRAGONFIRE

Welcome to the world of
MASK
MOBILE ARMOURED STRIKE KOMMAND

Imagine a world where there is more
to reality than meets the eye. Where
illusion and deception team up with
man and machine to create a world of
sophisticated vehicles and weaponry,
manned by agents and counter-agents.

Dragonfire

The MASK mission: to protect the
Temple of the Dragons from the vile
atrocities of the VENOM agents. Scott
Trakker and his robot companion
T-Bob find themselves again at the
forefront of an exciting story in an
exotic part of the world.

The eighth extraordinary MASK
adventure!

MATT TRAKKER – SPECTRUM

MATT TRAKKER – ULTRA FLASH

BRAD TURNER – HOCUS POCUS

HONDO MACLEAN – BLASTER

BUDDIE HAWKES – PENETRATOR

DUSTY HAYES – BACKLASH

BRUCE SATO – LIFTER

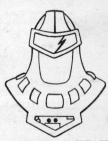

ALEX SECTOR – JACKRABBIT

CLIFF DAGGER – THE TORCH

MILES MAYHEM – VIPER

SLY RAX – STILETTO

MASK

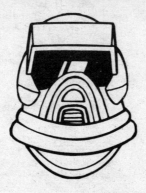

DRAGONFIRE

novelisation by
Kenneth Harper
Illustrated by Bruce Hogarth

KNIGHT BOOKS
Hodder and Stoughton

Text copyright © Kenneth Harper 1987
Illustrations copyright © Bruce Hogarth 1987

First published in Great Britain by Knight Books 1987

Mask TM and the associated trade marks are the property of Kenner Parker Toys Inc. (KPT) 1986
Second impression 1987

Printed and bound in Great Britain for Hodder and Stoughton Paperbacks, a division of Hodder and Stoughton Limited, Mill Road, Dunton Green, Sevenoaks, Kent (Editorial Office: 47 Bedford Square, London WC1B 3DP) by Cox & Wyman Limited, Reading, Berks. Photoset by Rowland Phototypesetting Limited, Bury St Edmunds, Suffolk.

British Library C.I.P.

Harper, Kenneth, *1940–*
    Dragonfire. – (Mask; 8).
    Rn: Keith Miles
    I. Title   II. Hogarth, Bruce
    III. Series
    823'.914[J]   PZ7

ISBN 0-340-41684-4

MASK

ONE

The island of Borneo was covered for the most part with tropical rain forests and jungle. There were extensive swampy lowlands to the south and southwest. But it had a mountainous interior and some of its peaks were quite forbidding.

A lush valley lay at the very heart of the country. It was surrounded by craggy mountains whose pinnacles disappeared into a heavy mist. A large thatched house stood in the valley and overlooked a plantation of cinchona trees. The veranda of the dwelling afforded a fine view of the impressive landscape.

Matt Trakker and his adopted son, Scott, enjoyed the scene from the veranda. With them were T-Bob, the boy's robot companion, and Julio Lopez, doctor and MASK agent. All four of them had come to Borneo in response to an invitation. They were delighted with all they saw.

Scott was particularly interested in the native who was working nearby. The man was carving slices of bark off a cinchona trunk and laying them carefully on a small rack.

'How about that!' said Scott in surprise. 'I never knew they made medicine out of *trees*!'

'That's how they get quinine,' explained Matt. 'There's enough in the bark of that cinchona to treat hundreds of malaria patients. Julio knows more about that than I do.'

'Yes,' added the MASK agent. 'What they do is to mix the bark with milk of lime, add boiling alcohol, then extract the alkaloid in the form of sulphate.'

'And you end up with quinine?' asked Scott.

'That's right,' replied Julio. 'It's a wonderful drug. There's no better way of fighting malaria.'

T-Bob's oblong mouth lit up as he spoke.

'I know *another* important thing doctors get from trees.'

'What's that?' said the boy.

'Tongue depressors!'

They all burst out laughing at the robot's joke.

It was at that point that Dr Munda entered with a native servant, Hatta, who carried a tray of drinks. Dr Munda was a big, robust man in his fifties with a great enthusiasm for his work. Hatta was a thin, shy native wearing little more than a loin-cloth.

8

'Sounds like everyone's having fun!' noted Dr Munda.

'Yes,' agreed Matt. 'T-Bob is keeping us amused.'

'I knew I *would* if I talked about trees,' observed the robot. 'Get it? Wood – trees!'

They all groaned at the dreadful pun.

Dr Munda indicated the tray of drinks.

'I thought you might like some refreshments.'

They all expressed their thanks and took a glass each.

'If there's anything else you'd like,' offered their host, 'just let me know.'

'As a matter of fact, there is,' said Julio. 'What I'd really like is a peek at your botany experiments.'

Dr Munda smiled and patted him on the shoulder.

'My pleasure, Julio. I'll show you around my laboratory after dinner.'

Before anyone else could speak, they were interrupted by a low rumble of thunder. Then there was a flash of lightning and the whole veranda was bathed for a split-second in a green hue. The visitors were at once surprised and alarmed.

'Wow!' exclaimed Scott. 'What was that?'

Thunder and lightning continued in the background.

'Hope it's not a storm,' bleated T-Bob. 'When it rains, my head leaks and my feet flood. I'm not waterproof.'

Dr Munda went to the edge of the veranda and gazed up.

'Mount Kinibalu is acting up again,' he said.

'Mount Kinibalu?' asked Matt.

His host pointed towards the distant crag.

'Over there, Matt. Across the valley. It's the tallest mountain in Borneo.'

His guests turned their attention to Mount Kinibalu. It dominated the rugged mountain range. Its peak was hidden beneath a dark, swirling mist that dropped down its upper slopes like a waterfall. The thunder and lightning seemed to be coming from directly above Mount Kinibalu.

Whenever the lightning flashed, a green glow covered the whole area. It was quite spectacular.

Dr Munda nodded towards the mist-shrouded summit.

'That peak is always covered by those greenish clouds,' he explained. 'The natives say they hide Kinibalu's secrets.'

The guests pricked up their ears with interest.

'What kind of secrets?' wondered Julio.

Dr Munda turned to his native servant.

'Perhaps you should tell them, Hatta . . .'

The servant came forward slowly. When more lightning flashed, he glanced up at the summit with obvious terror.

'Oh, is angry mountain!' he said, his voice trembling. 'Many people climb Kinibalu to find its secrets. No come back.'

'Why not?' asked Matt.

Thunder rolled once more and the lightning followed.

Hatta cowered in fear at it all.

'Thunder is roar of dragons!' he exclaimed. 'And the lightning is Dragonfire.' He raised a thin, shaking finger at the summit. 'See – it is *green*!'

Matt studied it and was completely baffled.

'Green lightning! Doesn't make sense.'

'Incredible!' added Julio.

'Dragons are angry with us,' insisted Hatta.

Scott Trakker turned excitedly to T-Bob.

'Oh boy! Wouldn't you love to meet a real fire-breathing dragon, T-Bob?'

'Are you crazy?' answered the robot. 'With my luck, I'd end up Kentucky fried T-Bob.'

The rumbling reached a new pitch of intensity.

'When it grows dark,' explained the frightened Hatta, 'the Dragonfire fills the sky.'

'It's true,' confirmed Dr Munda. 'I've seen it.'

A firework display of lightning exploded around the peak of the mountain. The green glow stretched for miles around.

'Old Kinibalu is sure acting up!' noted Julio. 'Wonder what's going on up there. Any guesses, Matt?'

'Not yet.'

'I'd like to find out what's happening.'

By way of an answer, Matt Trakker nodded thoughtfully. The legend about the dragons intrigued him. He wanted to learn the full truth about Kinibalu as well.

Before leaving Borneo, he would unravel the mystery.

It was a silent promise that he made to himself.

The Dyaks were a tribe of natives living in a primitive encampment some miles away. Their simple huts were arranged in a circle around a clearing in the thick vegetation. At the centre of their little village was their meeting place, a large hut built out of wood and thatch.

Chief Wadula was sitting on the ground talking to a few of the elders. Like Hatta, they were disturbed by the thunder and lightning that was coming from Kinibalu.

Then something happened which took their minds completely off the Dragonfire. They had some unexpected visitors.

Three strange vehicles arrived.

Instinct got Chief Wadula to his feet.

Danger threatened.

After an excellent meal that evening, Matt and the others were shown around Dr Munda's laboratory. It was an enormous greenhouse that had been built on at the back of the property. The expanse of glass was still gaining a lot of heat from the evening sun.

Dr Munda indicated an exotic-looking orchid.

'Now this specimen is particularly interesting,' he said.

'What's so special about it?' asked Julio.

'It appears to have the ability to sense danger and to take steps to avoid it. Watch.'

Dr Munda picked up a pair of garden shears near the orchid and opened the blades as if he was about to trim its leaves. The stem bent over quickly so that the leaves moved out of the way of the snapping shears.

'Fantastico!' announced Julio.

'Where did you find it?' questioned Matt.

'It grows in only one place,' said Dr Munda. 'On the slopes of Mount Kinibalu.'

'That mountain gets more and more interesting,' noted Matt.

Dr Munda walked around and indicated several other plants.

'That's where I've discovered most of these specimens. Almost all of them have amazing – even *magical* – properties.'

'Such as?' asked Julio.

His host gestured to a plant with long tendrils.

'This one here produces a sort of gum that is like honey. It is very good for curing aches and pains.' He pointed to another plant. 'That one has even greater medicinal value . . .'

Dr Munda went into great detail as he explained about his specimens. Matt and Julio were keen to hear him but much of the scientific jargon was beyond Scott. He and T-Bob drifted off to the other side of the laboratory.

'I've never seen any of these amazing looking plants before,' he confided. 'They're kinda weird.'

T-Bob nodded at a large tangled growth in a pot.

'Dig that!' he said then rocked with mirth.

It was cut short by a strange howl from outside.

'What was *that*!' shouted T-Bob.

'Sounded like it came from out there.'

Scott moved to the door and started to open it.

'Careful!' warned T-Bob. 'It could be a killer turnip!'

A second howl filled the air. The boy's curiosity was aroused now. Followed by T-Bob, he went through the door and found himself on a patio.

He found something else as well.

'Wow! T-Bob, will you look at that!'

'I don't believe it!'

'Do you see what *I* see!'

The creature let out another mournful howl.

It was a huge orang-utan.

TWO

'Ask it, Scott.'
'I don't spe
'All you
T-Bo
wi

The animal was in a large cage which stood in the middle of the patio. Tawny in colour, it sat listlessly on the floor and gazed out through the bars with sad eyes. Several uneaten bananas lay near the orang-utan. It clearly had no appetite.

Seeing Scott and T-Bob, the creature continued its howl.

'Awoooooooooh!'

Scott was immediately taken with the animal.

'Kinda cute, huh?'

'Cute?' repeated T-Bob, who was more cautious. 'Well, I'll say one thing – it's got a beautiful head of hair. All over its body!'

'Why doesn't it eat those bananas?'

…ak orang-utan.'

… have to say is – awoooooooooh!'

…ob's impersonation made the animal's eyes
…den.

'Awoooooooooh!' it replied.

'See?' boasted T-Bob. 'I picked up the lingo in one
go.'

They moved in closer to the cage. Dr Munda came
out on to the patio with Matt and Julio. He smiled
when he saw what had happened.

'So you've met Simbala, have you?'

'Is that his name, Dr Munda?' asked Scott.

'Not *his*,' explained the other. '*Hers*.'

'Oh,' said the boy. 'Simbala is a girl!'

'A full-grown lady, by the look of it,' observed Matt.

'Is she your pet, Dr Munda?' wondered Scott.

'No,' he replied. 'Some natives brought her to me.
She was injured while trying to defend her child
against a tiger.'

'That's too bad,' remarked Matt. 'Is the kid okay?'

'Don't know,' continued Munda. 'We can't find
it.'

'Why not?' said Julio.

'It escaped during the attack. Poor Simbala is heart-
broken. She never stops howling for her lost child.'

Right on cue, the orang-utan let out another cry.

'Awoooooooooooooh!'

'Is Simbala better now?' asked Scott.

'More or less,' said Dr Munda. 'We've nursed her

back to health. The only problem is that she won't eat enough. She's too upset most of the time.'

T-Bob looked at the animal with great compassion.

'*I* can cheer her up!' he decided.

'How, T-Bob?' said Scott.

'Like this . . . Simbala – watch me!'

The robot telescoped its arms out so that they touched the floor. Then he leapt about and scratched under his arms, emitting sounds that were very similar to those made by the animal.

'Awooo. Eeee. Eeeee. Yuh, yuh, yuh. Awooo!'

Simbala peered through her bars with intense concentration.

Scott led the laughter at the robot's antics.

'Keep it up, T-Bob!'

'Awooo. Eeee. Eeeee. Yuh, yuh, yuh. Awooo!'

He hopped around outside the cage and scratched even more furiously. T-Bob had certainly gained Simbala's attention.

'I told you I'd cheer her up!' boasted T-Bob.

But the robot had done far more than that. Not only had the orang-utan stopped howling. It was standing up inside its cage and gazing at the little metal figure with maternal affection.

T-Bob was like the baby that Simbala had lost.

'Awooo. Eeee. Eeeee. Yuh, yuh, yuh. Awooo!'

The robot moved in so that he was almost face to face with the tawny creature. He mimicked everything that Simbala did, acting like a reflection in a mirror.

When Simbala put her finger in her mouth, T-Bob

copied her. When she scratched her head, he followed suit again. When she let loose a stream of orang-utan chatter, he repeated it.

The adults were very amused by it all.

'Great stuff, T-Bob!' congratulated Matt.

'You're more orang-utan than *she* is,' said Julio.

'I'm just . . . keeping her up to scratch,' explained T-Bob, scratching under his arms again. 'This is dead easy! I'm a natural.'

'You're a regular ham, T-Bob!' teased Scott.

'Right,' agreed the robot. 'A canned ham!'

He went off into a hysterical giggle but it was short-lived. Simbala suddenly reached through the bars, took a firm grip on the robot and pulled him close.

T-Bob was frankly terrified and shook all over.

'Yipe!'

The others simply laughed at his predicament.

Simbala offered the robot a banana.

'Huh?' said T-Bob. 'No thanks. I don't want any bananas. They don't *appeal* to me.'

Scott and the others pulled a face at the awful pun.

Simbala ate half the banana then thrust the remainder of it at T-Bob. The robot turned its head away. Scott chuckled.

'What a pretty mother you have, T-Bob!'

'She's not my mother!' wailed his little friend.

'*You* know that,' said the boy. 'Simbala doesn't.'

The orang-utan embraced T-Bob warmly and gave

21

him a motherly kiss on the top of his head. He turned bright scarlet.

'Yuck!'

There was general hilarity all round.

Matt then took Dr Munda aside for a moment.

'Do you think you could keep an eye on Scott and T-Bob for a day or so?' he asked.

'Sure. No problem. Where are you going?'

'Julio and I want to get a closer look at this so-called "Dragonfire",' said Matt.

'I wouldn't advise it,' replied Dr Munda with concern.

'Why not?'

'There are mysteries about Mount Kinibalu that even *I* don't understand and I've been working here for ages.'

'Still like to check it out,' persisted Matt. 'As long as you don't mind Scott and T-Bob staying with you . . .'

'Not at all,' said Dr Munda. 'T-Bob's good for Simbala. He might help to speed her recovery.'

'He can do some baby-sitting for you with the orang-utan.'

'It's Scott who'll have to do that,' noted Dr Munda with a grin. 'Simbala has decided that *T-Bob* is the baby!'

The animal gave the robot another smacking kiss.

'Ugh!' yelled T-Bob in horror. 'Simbala is trying to make a monkey out of me.'

Happy laughter echoed up and down the valley.

Even the orang-utan joined in.

23

It was nightfall by the time they finally found out what they wanted. Leaving the Dyak village, they camped on the edge of the jungle. They were up again at dawn on the following morning.

Over breakfast, their leader outlined the plan.

'We'll go up there and steal the lot!'

It was Miles Mayhem, the ruthless boss of VENOM. With him were three of his toughest henchmen.

Sly Rax. Bruno Shepard. Floyd Malloy.

'How much you reckon is up there, Mayhem?' asked Bruno, a burly thug with a Mohican haircut. 'What kind of a haul?'

'It could be worth millions, Bruno.'

'Great! We'll be rich!'

'That money will buy us *power*!' asserted Mayhem, punching the air with his fist. 'We'll get more mercenaries and machines and deadly weapons. Then nobody will be able to stop us.'

'Not even MASK?' said Sly Rax.

'We'll wipe them out completely!' boasted the VENOM boss with an evil cackle. 'Then we'll have nothing standing between us and world domination. Just think of it, men. Miles Mayhem. Ruler of the whole world!'

'What will that make us?' asked Floyd with a sneer.

'My minions!'

'As long as we get our share of the loot,' grunted Rax.

'Yeah,' added Bruno. 'You can have the power, Mayhem. *We* want the dough!'

'You'll get it,' promised the VENOM leader, rubbing his hands together with glee. 'We're really going to hit the jackpot this time. And the great thing is that MASK doesn't have a chance of stopping us.'

'Why not?' asked Floyd, scratching his head.

'Because they're thousands of miles away, you idiot!' retorted Mayhem. 'Trakker and his men would never dream of coming anywhere like Borneo. We've got the island to ourselves. VENOM can clean up in a big way.'

Another evil cackle escaped his grinning mouth.

VENOM was at it again.

Anxious to make an early start, Matt Trakker and Julio Lopez left the house as dawn was breaking. Thunder Hawk was in sports car mode as it took them along a rough track through the jungle. Matt was driving. Julio, in the passenger seat, looked through the windscreen at Mount Kinibalu in the middle distance. It was still wreathed in the green mist.

'I can't figure out that green haze,' admitted Julio.

'Just as well T-Bob's not here,' commented Matt.

'Why?'

'He'd tell us it was *myst*erious!'

Julio tried to ignore the joke.

'Any idea what we'll find up there, Matt?'

'I haven't the foggiest.'

His companion could not resist a smile this time.

'I asked for that,' he conceded.

Matt Trakker studied the mountain and became serious.

'One thing's for sure, Julio. I don't buy that story about the dragons. Poor old Hatta was frightened out of his skin when the lightning flashed above Kinibalu. He thinks it's the dragons. I believe there's a simpler explanation.'

'And what is it?'

Before Matt could reply, they were diverted by sounds off to their right. They had reached the village in the jungle clearing and could see the Dyaks running around in confusion.

The meeting place had been destroyed.

'Looks like trouble,' decided Matt. 'Let's check it out.'

MASK swung into action once again.

THREE

Thunder Hawk screeched to a halt in front of the smoking ruin of the meeting house. Matt Trakker and Julio Lopez jumped out and went across to Chief Wadula. The old native's face was pitted with anxiety and pain. He was clearly in a state of shock.

'What happened?' asked Matt.

'It was horrible!' exclaimed the Chief.

'Tell us,' urged Julio.

'Bad men came. Tried to make me tell them where on Mount Kinibalu is Temple of Dragons?'

'Temple of Dragons?' repeated Matt.

'The sacred place of my people,' explained Chief Wadula. 'Built many years ago by our gods. When me no tell bad men the truth, they destroy our meeting place with boom-boom!'

The MASK agents looked at the heap of rubble. No wonder the tribesmen were so upset. Their communal building had been utterly wrecked by the unwelcome visitors.

Matt was determined to help in every way he could.

'Can you describe what they look like?' he asked.

'These bad men?' said the Chief.

'Yes. Were they big, strong guys who pushed you around?'

'Afraid so. Can not see their faces, though.'

'Why not?' pressed Matt.

'Wear strange masks.'

'*Masks!*'

Matt Trakker exchanged a worried look with Julio Lopez.

It was beginning to sound like VENOM.

'If it *was* them,' noted Julio, 'they sure meant business.'

'They always do!' sighed Matt.

He took a closer look at the ruined meeting house and sifted through the rubble. Something caught his attention.

'The entire building is perforated with tiny holes,' he concluded. 'That's putting in air conditioning the hard way!'

Julio, meanwhile, had found something on the ground.

'Take a look, Matt.'

'What are they?'

'Ball bearings. See for yourself.'

Matt took them from him and examined them carefully.

His face darkened and he nodded soulfully.

'Yep. No doubt about it. This is the exact same type that Floyd Malloy uses in his Buckshot mask.' He turned back to the Chief. 'Did one of the bad men aim his mask at the meeting house?'

'Yes!' said Chief Wadula sadly.

'That proves it was VENOM!'

'VENOM?' echoed the old native.

'Vicious Evil Network of Mayhem,' explained Matt. 'It's a highly dangerous criminal organization and they've got to be stopped. Otherwise, they'll raid your temple.'

'Don't let them do that!' pleaded the Chief.

'Tell us where it is,' said Julio. 'We'll make sure that VENOM won't steal anything from you.'

Chief Wadula was not altogether reassured.

'There were *four* of them and they had powerful weapons,' he remembered. 'There are only two of you.'

'We'll bring in a support team,' promised Matt. 'Now give us all the details . . .'

A few minutes later, Thunder Hawk was haring along the rough track in the direction of Mount Kinibalu. Still driving, Matt punched a button to activate the computer.

He snapped a command into the microphone.

31

'Select the MASK agents best-suited for this mission!'

The screen flashed with static for a few moments and then it showed a face along with computer graphics of a specialist vehicle. As usual, the computer voice was calm, crisp and female.

'Recommended personnel. Brad Turner, expert mountain climber. Civilian job: rock musician. Vehicle code name: Condor.'

'Approved!' said Matt.

Another face and vehicle appeared on the screen.

'Gloria Baker, black belt in Kung Fu. Former student of anthropology. Vehicle code name: Shark.'

'Approved.'

The screen scrambled then cleared once more. The face that now came into view was the one sitting alongside Matt.

'Julio Lopez. Pre-selected. Doctor in family medicine. Vehicle code name: Firefly.'

'Personnel approved!' announced Matt. 'Assemble Mobile Armoured Strike Kommand! We'll rendezvous with the MASK hovercraft on Mount Kinibalu!'

As he gave the orders, Matt pressed the button on his watch. The word MASK showed on the liquid crystal display. It was the pre-arranged signal for all MASK agents.

They were crack troops in the fight against evil.

Their response would be immediate.

Brad Turner was relaxing on a couch in his home. He was wearing a headset and listening to some rock music on his highly expensive stereo equipment. His foot was tapping in time to the music and he snapped his fingers.

Suddenly, his watch bleeped and flashed.

Without pausing for an instant, Brad leapt up from the couch and ran towards the door. He completely forgot that he had the headset on. He moved so fast that the cable yanked the stereo equipment on to the floor.

In an emergency, such things were expendable.

Gloria Baker, meanwhile, was in the middle of a Kung Fu class. Wearing judo kit, she circled her opponent warily and looked for an opening. She was taking on a big, powerfully-built man and there was a knot of spectactors cheering her on.

Before they could grapple, she received her call on the MASK watch. At that moment, her opponent decided to make his move. He lunged at her with all his might. But Gloria was no longer there. Reacting to the signal, she sprinted away without explanation.

Her opponent was left clutching fresh air. His impetus carried him on and he landed in the lap of a fat woman in the front row of the spectators.

The two MASK agents made their way at top speed to their secret headquarters at the Boulder Hill Gas Station. When they had gone through their rituals, they stored their vehicles in the hovercraft.

They were soon racing across the sky towards Borneo.

Help was on its way.

T-Bob sat on the ground near the cage and wearily peeled a banana. As the first slice of peel was pulled down, he talked to himself.

'She loves me . . .'

Another slice of the skin was peeled down.

'She loves me not . . .'

He pulled down the final piece of banana skin.

'She *loves* me . . . Ugh!' The robot tossed the banana away quickly. He was surrounded by dozens of other bananas. As he had unpeeled them, they all gave him the same answer. T-Bob turned back to the orangutan.

Simbala tossed him another banana and blew him a kiss.

'Stop that!' he protested. 'I'm not *your* kid. I'm a robot. Do I *look* like a monkey!'

Watching from nearby, Scott had a fit of giggles.

'And *you* can shut up as well!' said T-Bob.

'Simbala's really gone ape over you,' teased Scott. 'Looks like she wants you to move into her cage.'

T-Bob drew back at once from the bars.

'I'm not moving anywhere!' he declared.

But the decision was taken out of his hands. As he stepped back, he trod on a banana skin and it sent him flying through the air. He let out an ear-splitting shriek.

'Whoah!!!!'

T-Bob landed on the cage and his legs and arms wrapped themselves round the bars. Simbala obviously thought her "child" was trying to get to her. She put her arms through the bars and embraced the robot in a warm hug.

Simbala emitted a stream of orang-utan chatter.

T-Bob, meanwhile, struggled madly to get free.

'Get your hairy arms off me!'

'Momma wants you!' mocked Scott, shaking with mirth.

'Yow!' exclaimed T-Bob. 'Simbala's got a crush on me!'

The orang-utan kissed him on the head then started to rock him to and fro as if singing him a lullaby. The rocking became more and more violent until the whole cage was on the move.

Scott stopped laughing. The situation became much more serious. Simbala rocked the cage so hard that it tipped right over and snapped off at the base.

The orang-utan was now free.

She grabbed T-Bob up in her arms and held him tight.

'Scott – save me!' yelled the robot in desperation.

'I'm coming, T-Bob!'

The boy took a firm grip on his friend's arm and pulled. But Simbala was not going to surrender her "child" as easily as that. She resisted the pull. Scott and the orang-utan became engaged in a tug-of-war, using T-Bob as the rope.

'Yiiiiiiiii!' howled the robot.

'I'll rescue you!' promised the boy.

But his strength was no match for that of Simbala. With one final pull, she shook Scott off and tucked T-Bob under her arm. Running on the outsides of her feet, she then padded quickly across the patio and headed for the trees.

T-Bob was now hoarse with terror.

'Heeeeeeeeelp!'

'Stop, Simbala!' shouted Scott.

'Put me down, Momma!' pleaded the robot.

'Hold on, T-Bob!' urged Scott. 'I'll get you out of this!'

'I hope so! Follow that ape!'

Simbala moved faster and faster towards the trees.

Scott ran after her as quickly as he could.

It was no joke any longer.

T-Bob had been kidnapped!

FOUR

Matt Trakker and Julio Lopez continued on their journey towards Mount Kinibalu. Still in sports car mode, Thunder Hawk took them along a winding track through the jungle. As they got closer to their destination, green mist began to float down and envelop them.

Occasional thunder rumbled. Green lightning flashed.

'There it goes again!' observed Julio.

'I just don't believe it!' protested Matt. 'I mean, who ever heard of *green* lightning?'

'Seeing is believing, Matt.'

'Unless it's some kind of optical illusion.'

The mist thickened around them and they had to

slow down. When the haze cleared, they found themselves near the slope of Mount Kinibalu. Stretching out in front of them was a field of beautiful flowers. The sight was breathtaking.

'Wow!' said Matt. 'What a garden!'

'Flowers!' noted Julio. 'There're thousands of 'em.' He turned to his leader. 'Hey, maybe *that's* what Mayhem's after!'

'You could be right, Julio,' agreed Matt. 'Dr Munda said the plants on Mount Kinibalu had magical properties. VENOM wants to get its evil hands on them!'

'Why don't I take a closer look?'

'Fine.'

Matt brought Thunder Hawk to a juddering halt. Julio got out and walked across the field. Flowers of all kinds and colours surrounded him. He was entranced by it all.

Julio then took a deep breath and filled his lungs.

'Mmmm! They sure smell great!'

He went further into the field and was soon swallowed up by the green mist that came rolling down the slope of Kinibalu.

Matt lowered a window to call to his colleague.

'See anything interesting, Julio?'

There was no reply. Matt became rather anxious.

'Julio! Where are you, Julio?'

Still no answer. He strained his eyes to see through the mist but it was hopeless. Opening the door, he got out of Thunder Hawk and went to find Julio.

The field was now one great sea of mist.

'Can you hear me!' he shouted. 'It's Matt! Where are you?'

Thunder rolled and green lightning penetrated the mist. It enabled Matt to see Julio. The MASK agent was lying face downwards on the ground as if unconscious. Matt ran to him.

'Julio!'

A tired groan was all that the other could manage. 'Ohhhhhh . . .'

'What happened!' wondered Matt.

He looked around the immediate vicinity. The ground was covered with tiny puffball plants. Tucked in amongst them were various human skulls and bones. There was even part of the skeleton of a cow. Matt picked up the skull of a human head.

Was this one of the people who had come to Kinibalu in search of its secrets? Had the mountain claimed his life?

'We've got a grave situation here,' commented Matt.

As he picked up some of the bones, a puffball exploded silently near his face, releasing a rush of sleep-inducing vapour.

Matt was affected at once. He felt weak all over and his head began to swim. He pointed down at the puffballs.

'The flowers! They're poison!'

Julio had obviously been laid low the same way.

Matt dropped the skull and the bones. Grabbing hold of the prostrate figure of Julio, he tried vainly to

drag him towards Thunder Hawk. They had to escape.

'Must get back to . . .'

The words trailed away as his strength faded. Other puffballs now exploded and sent up fresh supplies of the knockout gas. Matt did his best to struggle against it.

'Can't give up . . . I . . .'

But it was too overpowering. Before he had gone another step, he succumbed to the poison and drifted off into a deep sleep. Matt and Julio lay side by side in the field, covered by the mist.

MASK was out for the count.

T-Bob had never felt so frightened or so dizzy in all his days. He was tucked under Simbala's long arm as she used the other to swing through the trees. The ground was about fifteen metres below them.

'Save me!' screeched the robot.

'Here I come!' yelled Scott.

He had climbed a tree himself and taken hold of a creeper. It was his chance to play Tarzan. Banging his chest and uttering the cry of the King of the Apes, the boy swung on the creeper and landed on the highest branch of the next tree.

'Hey!' he exclaimed. 'I'm getting the *hang* of this!'

He grabbed another creeper and set off again.

T-Bob, meanwhile, was suffering agonies.

'Don't drop me, Simbala!' he begged. 'I'm too young to die!'

'I'll catch you up!' shouted Scott.

'Then *hurry*!' implored the robot. 'I don't have a head for heights. I hate it when someone monkeys around with me!'

Simbala now swung to another tree before adjusting her hold on her "child". T-Bob found himself turned upside down.

'How's it going, T-Bob?' called Scott, still in pursuit.

'Things are not looking up!' he wailed.

Scott paused to get his breath back and realized what was happening. The orang-utan was swinging towards the misty foothills of Mount Kinibalu. The boy sensed danger at once.

He cupped his hands to bellow after the robot.

'You got to stop her, T-Bob. She's taking you up Kinibalu!'

'Oh no!'

The mist enfolded them and thunder roared. The lightning flashed with dramatic effect and bathed everything in green once more. T-Bob was now gibbering.

'The Dragonfire! Not that! Please!'

'I'll find you!' promised Scott. 'Just keep yelling!'

The robot needed no encouragement to do that.

'That's one thing I'm great at! Yiiiiiiii!'

The mist had thickened so much now that Scott had lost sight of them completely. He swung to a tree then paused on a bough.

'Which way are you headed, T-Bob?'

At that moment, Simbala landed on a branch that

was too thin to take the combined weight of herself and T-Bob. As it broke, the orang-utan tried to steady herself. In a moment of panic, she grabbed for the trunk with both hands. The robot slipped out from beneath her arm and fell through the air.

Scott's voice cut through the thick mist.

'T-Bob! Tell me where you're going!'

The robot had the answer to that.

'STRAIGHT DOOOOOOOOOWN!'

His voice got smaller as he rocketed earthwards. Then there was a dull thud as he hit the ground. Simbala was inconsolable. She peered down from her perch at the top of the tree but she could see nothing. Her mournful howl was heard again.

'Awoooooooooh!'

T-Bob did not hear the cry. He was too busy trying to work out if he was still in one piece. Although the fall had been a long one, he had made a soft landing on a pile of leaves. He shook his arms and legs to make sure that they were still attached to his body, then he stood up and conducted a more thorough examination.

He found a shallow dent in his chest.

'Whew!' he whistled with relief. 'Lucky me! Just one small dent. We'll soon take care of that.'

A lid opened on his head and out popped a steel suction pad on the end of a long arm. The pad fixed itself to T-Bob's chest and there was an electronic hum.

'Oo!' he laughed. 'It tickles!'

The dent was lifted out in no time at all. When the arm had retracted inside his head, the lid closed with a

clang. T-Bob was delighted with the on-the-spot re-pair.

'Hey presto! Good as new!'

He tried to decide where he was, but the mist was far too dense. T-Bob could hardly see a hand in front of his face.

He gulped in fear.

'It's one of those pea soup fogs – without the soup!'

Moving gingerly, he started to walk forwards. Be-cause the visibility was so bad, he went straight into another tree.

'Sorry!' he apologized. 'Fancy bumping into you!'

Arms held out in front of him to ward off danger, he staggered on. Being held under Simbala's arm had been terrifying enough, but this was worse. He was lost and alone.

'Scott!' he piped. 'Scott!'

The ground began to fall away beneath his feet and he realized that he was on the slope of the mountain.

'Guess if I head downhill, I'll run into *someone*!'

His prediction came true almost immediately.

As he blundered on through the mist, he tripped over a solid object and was hurled to the ground with a bump.

'What was *that*!'

He crawled back to the solid object and saw that it was Matt Trakker. He and Julio Lopez were still lying side by side among the poisonous puffballs.

'Julio! Matt! What happened to you guys?'

He shook them hard but all they could do was groan.

'This place is not healthy!' decided the robot. 'I'll get you out of here. Lie still and leave it to me.'

He extended an arm to pick Matt up and drop him on to his shoulder. Then he lifted Julio on to his other shoulder. With the two MASK agents as his luggage, he trudged slowly on.

'If only I had some help!' he croaked.

It was nearer at hand than he imagined. Scott heard his voice and called back to him through the mist.

'T-Bob, is that you?'

'Yes!'

'Try to hold on! I'm coming!'

'Thank goodness for that!'

They made their way towards each other through the gloom. T-Bob was not able to walk very fast with his burden, but Scott was even slower. Puffballs were exploding everywhere and sending up clouds of poisonous vapour. He was soon overwhelmed by it.

He staggered right up to T-Bob.

'Hello, Scott. What kept you?'

The boy's legs began to buckle and his voice was slurred.

'I feel . . . so sleepy!'

He slumped to the ground and lay at the robot's feet.

'Welcome to T-Bob's slumber party!'

Now he had *three* sleeping friends to help.

'I'd better convert to scooter mode!' he decided.

The wheels appeared at once and his back extended to take a passenger. Using both arms, he lifted Scott up and draped him over the seat. Then he adjusted Matt and Julio on his shoulders before setting off at a sedate pace.

The last thing he wanted was to collide with another tree.

Puffballs exploded all around him and the air was charged with the sleeping gas. But T-Bob was immune to it. Since he had no sense of smell and no lungs, he could not be affected by any nasal poison. Matt, Julio and Scott moaned gently, but T-Bob felt fine. It would take more than a puffball to puff him over.

Simbala continued to howl from her treetop.

'Awoooooooooh!'

'Sorry, Momma!' said T-Bob. 'But I'm needed here.'

He followed the incline downwards so that he was moving away from Mount Kinibalu but the mist did not clear. Instead, it seemed to get thicker than ever.

T-Bob looked around in utter dismay.

'At least I'm not *kinda* lost any more,' he decided. 'I'm completely lost.'

He rolled on slowly with his three passengers.

It was vital to get them away from the poison.

FIVE

Three VENOM vehicles made their way up the winding road to the summit of Mount Kinibalu. Scorpion, the armoured limousine, was at the front of the procession. It was driven by Bruno Shepard who had Miles Mayhem as his passenger. Behind them were Sly Rax on Piranha, his motorcycle and sidecar; and Floyd Malloy on Vampire, his red high-powered motorbike. Rax was wearing his usual dark glasses and Floyd's long fair hair was streaming in the wind.

They were making slow progress because there were so many obstructions on the road. As they rounded a bend, another hazard appeared up ahead of them. It was a massive boulder.

Bruno Shepard glared at it then roared a protest.

'Crud! Another boulder!'

'Get rid of it!' ordered Mayhem.

'Shall I try to find some way round it?'

'No. We're too close to the peak to detour now.'

Bruno nodded then pressed a series of buttons. Scorpion converted to battle mode. Its boot opened and its stinger claw was extended on a steel arm. The claw took a firm grip on the boulder and flung it aside. As it landed again, it almost hit Floyd, who had to swerve Vampire out of the way.

Scorpion converted back to car mode. Floyd Malloy drove angrily up to the passenger side of the car and spoke to Mayhem.

'Why'd you have Bruno throw that boulder at me!'

'Get off it!' sneered Bruno. 'You just have a habit of always getting in the way! You little runt!'

'I'm not a runt!' bellowed Floyd.

'Yes, you are!'

'Take that back, Bruno!'

'Never!'

'Nobody calls me a "runt" and gets away with it!'

Mayhem had had enough of the bickering. He turned to Floyd Malloy and subjected him to a withering gaze.

'Shut up – *runt*!'

Floyd glared resentfully but said nothing. Mayhem was the boss. He had to be obeyed. The VENOM leader jabbed a finger at the road ahead.

'Get going! We've had enough delays!'

Scorpion set off and led the way once again.

Green mist still shrouded the peak of Kinibalu. Every so often, thunder rolled and lightning set everything ablaze.

Miles Mayhem rubbed his hands together with glee.

'Waiting up there is the luckiest find of my life!' he said. 'The Temple of Dragons. It's where the natives keep all their secret treasures!'

The thunder and lightning intensified.

Mayhem's face was now bright green with avarice. 'Soon the Temple's riches will be mine!'

VENOM drove on towards its latest source of plunder.

Scott Trakker was the last to regain consciousness. As his mind slowly cleared and his eyes opened again, he thought he was back in the misty field of puffballs, trying to save T-Bob and Matt.

'Don't worry, T-Bob. I'm coming, Dad. Hold on.'

'Take it easy,' advised a soothing voice.

Scott blinked and saw Matt beaming down at him. Julio Lopez and T-Bob were there as well. They were still in the foothills of Kinibalu but there was no mist now. The boy was lying on the grass in a clearing. A stream meandered along nearby.

Scott was still a little groggy after his experience.

'Huh! Where am I?'

'Safe and sound,' said Julio.

'You had a close call,' explained Matt. 'So did we. Those puffballs contained a sleeping gas. If we hadn't been brought out into the fresh air, we'd have died there and added a few more bones to that collection.' He indicated the robot. 'T-Bob saved our lives.'

'Yes,' agreed Julio. 'He was magnificent. He carried all three of us out of that place of death.'

Scott got up and embraced the robot gratefully.

'T-Bob! You're a hero!'

'A hero!' repeated the other. 'But I was so *scared*! My *shocks* are still in shock!'

'How do you feel now, Scott?' asked Matt.

'Fine, Dad. Raring to go!'

'We were all pretty lucky,' observed Julio. 'Those flowers almost did us in.'

'Well,' said Matt, smiling. 'When you joined MASK, I never promised you a rose garden!'

Their laughter was interrupted by a humming sound.

Scott looked excitedly up to the sky.

'Hey! It's the MASK transport!'

'Hurrah!' cheered T-Bob. 'The cavalry has arrived!'

The transport vehicle swooped down out of the blue and positioned itself about eighty metres above the clearing. Its cargo door opened and Brad Turner emerged on Condor. His sleek motorcycle had converted to helicopter mode and he flew the vehicle to the ground.

'Hi, everybody!' he called. 'Where's the party?'

Another cargo door now opened in the transport and a cable system lowered down both Firefly and Shark. The two MASK vehicles were in car mode.

Gloria Baker sat at the controls of Shark and looked keen for action.

'Welcome to Borneo, Gloria!' said Matt.

'Thanks,' she replied. 'Where's VENOM?'

'We'll find him!' vowed the MASK leader.

Julio jumped into Firefly. Matt, Scott and T-Bob climbed into Thunder Hawk. The other three vehicles lined up in formation behind their leader.

Matt gave the command over the intercom.

'Let's go! It's time to ruin Mayhem's day!'

They sped off towards the green mist that curled around the upper reaches of Kinibalu. Having delivered its cargo, the transport craft now closed its doors and flew away.

Scott was delighted to be involved in it all.

'Thanks for letting us come along, Dad.'

'Well,' said Matt. 'With all those poison plants out there, you'll be much safer with me.'

'Just think!' mused the boy. 'We may get to see those fire-breathing dragons after all.'

'I don't want to see any dragons,' said T-Bob. 'Smoking is hazardous to my health.'

Matt and Scott laughed. Then they heard a familiar howl.

'Awoooooooooh!'

It was Simbala.

She was watching them from a treetop and she obviously recognized T-Bob. The orang-utan cried once more and used a vine to get to the next tree.

Matt was highly amused by the situation.

'Looks like T-Bob's mom is back in the swing of things!'

'Get me away from here!' yelled the robot. 'I'm not being carried off by an ape again!'

Thunder Hawk swept on past Simbala and she howled anew.

She followed the MASK vehicles at her own pace.

The orang-utan wanted her baby back.

The steep mountain trail finally levelled out and the VENOM vehicles came to a halt. They were facing the Temple of Dragons. It was a majestic structure in pagoda style, built entirely out of lustrous, gleaming green jade. There was a small lake beside it, reflecting its glories. The green mist cascaded down from the peak to swirl around the temple.

A slight drizzle fell. Lightning flashed and illuminated both the temple and the large open courtyard that was surrounded by massive jade pillars. It was an inspiring sight.

The VENOM agents stood agog at the wonder.

Miles Mayhem cackled with evil pleasure.

'A masterpiece! What a magnificent work of art!' He used the intercom to bark an order. 'Tear it down!'

Scorpion converted back into battle mode.

'The entire temple is made of jade,' continued Mayhem. 'It'll be worth a fortune on the black market.' He chuckled. 'Especially the dragons.'

Bruno Shepard felt cold tingles up his spine.

'Come on,' he said nervously. 'There really ain't no fire-breathing dragons around here . . . Right?'

'Of course not!' replied Mayhem.

As he spoke, more lightning flashed. A green glow spread everywhere for a few seconds and the VENOM vehicles changed colour.

'See?' explained Mayhem. 'The Dragonfire is ordinary lightning reflected off the jade temple. That's why it looks green. Those natives back there have been fooled all these years.'

'But you weren't fooled,' noted Bruno.

'Miles Mayhem is *never* fooled!'

Floyd Malloy went past on Vampire and entered the courtyard. He came to a dead halt and his blood froze. In the middle of the courtyard was the massive head of a giant dragon. Its eyes glared right at him and sparkled with malice.

'What the . . . !'

Floyd was so startled, he swung Vampire round and drove straight out of the yard, colliding with a bush as he did so. Grabbing his microphone, he yelled a warning to the others.

'A dragon! I saw it! It's inside! It's huge! And even uglier than Bruno!'

'What do you mean!' growled Bruno angrily.

Miles Mayhem was not alarmed by the warning.

'That's the *real* reason we're here,' he confided. 'I want that dragon. Drive on.'

Bruno took Scorpion through the archway and into the courtyard. Dominating the whole area was an

immense jade dragon head. It was so well carved that it looked completely lifelike. The glistening eyes which had scared off Floyd Malloy were in fact huge jewels.

'The finest, purest jade in the world!' announced Mayhem. 'It'll easily bring in ten thousand dollars. Rip it out!'

True to its name, Scorpion had its sting in its tail. The boot opened and its claw swung out.

'Now I'll show you one of my favourite old wrestling holds,' boasted Bruno at the controls. 'A headlock!'

The claw moved forward and closed on one of the dragon's enormous teeth. Lifting upwards, the claw pulled the dragon head off its base and held it in mid-air. Neither Mayhem nor Bruno noticed that a square hole had been uncovered in the ground.

'Take it outside,' ordered Mayhem. 'And be careful.'

As Scorpion headed for the entrance, Piranha and Vampire came tearing into the courtyard. They screamed to a halt.

'Big trouble!' exclaimed Rax.

'Yeah!' agreed Floyd. 'We've got company out there.'

Mayhem peered through the archway and saw the vehicles that were approaching. He hissed with annoyance.

'MASK!'

Another battle would soon commence.

SIX

VENOM had the advantage of surprise. Inside Scorpion, masks lowered automatically on to the heads of Mayhem and Bruno. Sly Rax and Floyd Malloy were also masked in readiness.

Mayhem snarled into the intercom.

'Keep them away from the temple at all costs!'

'What are we going to do?' asked Bruno.

'Set an ambush!'

The VENOM vehicles drove across the courtyard and lurked in the shadow of the walls. They were completely hidden from view.

MASK would be walking into a trap.

Further down the road, Thunder Hawk was still

forging ahead of its three support vehicles. All machines were in civilian mode.

They got their first sight of the dazzling temple.

'It's beautiful!' said Matt in admiration.

'Wow!' added Scott. 'I never saw a building so *green*!'

T-Bob was trembling with nerves at the thought of dragons.

'Yeah, why don't we come back some other time – when it *ripens* and turns yellow!'

Inside Firefly, Julio scrutinized the edifice.

'No sign of VENOM around the temple,' he said.

'But *plenty* of signs down there,' countered Matt.

He pointed to the assorted tracks on the ground. They had obviously been left by enemy vehicles. It was all the proof that Matt Trakker needed. His mask descended automatically.

Taking control, he issued his command.

'Let's get ready for them! Defence mode!'

They increased their speed towards the temple and converted into defence mode. Thunder Hawk's doors swung out to become gull-like wings and the vehicle became airborne. Condor followed suit. As the motorcycle gained its rotor blades, Brad Turner took to the sky in his one-man helicopter.

Shark and Firefly now had their defensive armoury and their weapons were trained for action. Gloria Baker and Julio Lopez were as eager as the others to fight it out with VENOM.

Scott Trakker was the most eager of them all.

'Isn't it exciting, T-Bob!' he shouted.

'No!' wailed the robot.

'We're gonna see all the action!'

'That's what worries me.'

'We got the best seats in the house.'

'Wouldn't it be better if we left early and beat the crowd?' suggested T-Bob.

'No! I don't want to miss any of the fun.'

'FUN!'

Gloria spoke to Matt over the intercom.

'Not a glimpse of VENOM yet. Are you sure they're here?'

'Quite sure!' insisted Matt.

'How can you be so certain?'

'I got this feeling. They'll show their hand soon.'

Matt Trakker was right yet again. The VENOM vehicles suddenly roared out of the courtyard in battle mode. They headed straight towards their mortal enemies.

Scott was both alarmed and delighted.

'Oh boy!' he said. 'Here we go!'

T-Bob put his hands over his eyes and ducked his head.

'Let me know when it's all over!'

Miles Mayhem took stock of the situation. Seated in the roof panel cockpit, he spotted that Gloria Baker was coming up fast.

'There's Shark!' he growled. 'Hold her back!'

Bruno Shepard punched a button on the console. Scorpion's tyre-mounted laser pods rotated and shot a

series of bolts at the oncoming MASK vehicle. They went right across Gloria's path and acted like an invisible barrier.

Shark tried to manoeuvre itself around the bolts but they only intensified. Gloria found that her vehicle was being forced back as if by a giant hand.

'Scorpion sure is pushy!' she said. 'Well, I'll just have to try another approach.'

The laser blast continued. Instead of trying to resist it, Shark turned around and went straight off the road. With a great splash, the vehicle plunged into the lake and vanished beneath the surface of the water.

Shark lived up to its name and converted at once to submarine mode. As it surged along underwater, it was tracked by Scorpion along the bank of the lake.

Mayhem was enraged because she had escaped him.

'Find her!' he bellowed.

Shark surfaced without warning and sped through the water at such speed that it sent up a huge wave in its wake.

'Try riding *this* wave, Mayhem!' said Gloria.

Scorpion tried to retreat but it was all to no avail. The wave soon overtook the vehicle and drenched it. Mayhem was splashed all over from head to foot. He spat water out through the openings in his mask.

'Get back to the temple!' he gurgled.

'Scorpion isn't built for swimming lessons,' agreed Bruno.

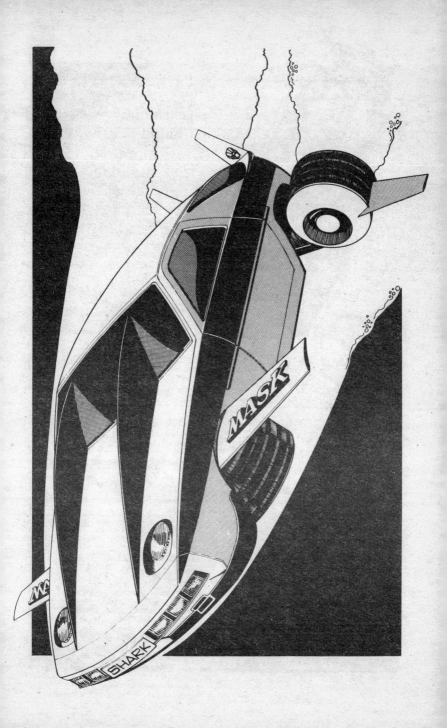

Mayhem switched on the intercom to contact Floyd Malloy.

'Vampire!'

'Yeah?'

'Cover us!'

'Check!'

Scorpion beat a hasty retreat as Vampire soared up into the sky. Floyd was in a confident mood. He surveyed the scene of battle and could not resist a boast.

'I'll do more than "cover",' he promised. 'I'll bring them to a dead halt!'

Vampire shot two of its retro-rockets at Thunder Hawk as the MASK vehicle swooped down towards it. The rockets attached themselves magnetically to each of Thunder Hawk's wings.

It came to an abrupt stop and stalled.

'What's going on!' asked Scott anxiously.

'Trouble!' admitted Matt, struggling with the controls.

'We're not flying any more!' bleated T-Bob.

'We've been retro-stopped!' conceded Matt.

'So what happens now?' said Scott in a worried voice. 'We can't just hang here in mid-air.'

They did not. Thunder Hawk started to fall.

It seemed to be heading for a terrible crash.

'Heeeeeeeeelp!' cried T-Bob.

'Don't be frightened,' said Scott, trying to be brave.

'We'll escape somehow,' vowed Matt.

He kept flicking switches on the console but

Thunder Hawk did not respond. The retro-rockets had disabled her completely.

The vehicle hurtled helplessly downwards.

Then Brad Turner decided to lend a hand.

'I'll put a start to that stop!' he said.

Condor's belly cannons fired lasers with the utmost precision. They knocked Vampire's magnetic retro-rockets off the wings of Thunder Hawk. The MASK vehicle immediately righted itself and came out of its plunge. Regaining control, Matt Trakker took them back up into the air to continue the battle.

He was keen to get his revenge.

Miles Mayhem led the retreat into the courtyard. Scorpion covered her withdrawal by firing lasers from her wheel pods. Vampire and Piranha were also finding MASK too hot to handle. They both came speeding back through the archway, their cannons still roaring.

Mayhem spoke to both agents over the intercom.

'Rax – Floyd – keep firing at them!'

'We'll hold 'em off!' replied Rax.

'Yeah,' said Floyd. 'Come and get us, MASK!'

They guarded the entrance to the courtyard and kept up a steady barrage of laser fire. It was enough to beat off the MASK vehicles for the time being.

But the real danger was not in front of Piranha and Vampire.

It was behind them!

When Scorpion had grabbed the jade dragon head

from its position, they had unwittingly lifted the lid on a deep pit. It was the lair of the guardians of the temple. Hearing the sounds of battle, those guardians now came out to investigate.

They were huge, powerful creatures with scales all over them. They had long necks and tails and forked tongues darted out of their mouths. Climbing out of their pit, they moved silently on large, clawed feet.

Nobody from the VENOM team saw or heard them.

Sly Rax was still near the archway, sitting on Piranha and firing lasers at the enemy. He suddenly felt something very warm directly behind him.

'Stop breathing down my neck, Floyd!' he said angrily.

The hot air continued to disturb him. Rax swung round in a temper to confront Floyd Malloy. Instead of seeing his VENOM colleague, however, he was eye to eye with one of the guardians of the temple.

His voice rose above the level of the combat.

'Yooooooooooooow!'

The creature lifted its legs and bared its great claws.

'Draaaaaaaaagons!' yelled Rax.

He swung Piranha to the right and drove off at breakneck speed towards a side exit in the courtyard. As he shot past Scorpion, his leader caught sight of him.

'Rax! Get back there with Floyd!'

Mayhem then understood why his henchman was beating a retreat. One of the monster lizards came up

to Scorpion and opened its jaws wide. Mayhem took one look into the gaping mouth.

'Aaaaaaaaaaargh!'

'A real dragon!' cried Bruno in terror.

'Get us outa here! Quick!'

Scorpion escaped in the nick of time. As it roared away, the creature's jaws snapped shut.

More giant lizards had crawled out of the pit now and they sloped across towards Floyd Malloy. As their shadows fell across him, he turned to see them. His courage failed him.

'Eeeeeeeeeeeeeh!'

Vampire tore off after the other VENOM vehicles.

The battle was well and truly over.

The villains had quit the field empty-handed.

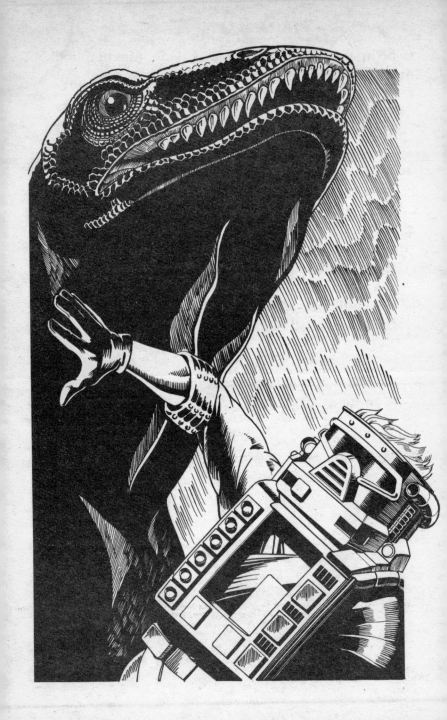

SEVEN

Matt Trakker and his team could not understand it.
VENOM had turned tail for no apparent reason. It was
not like them to run away from a fight until they could
see they were beaten.

Brad Turner scratched his head in puzzlement.

'What's with VENOM?' he asked.

The MASK team soon got their answer. As they
closed in on the temple, they saw the creatures crawl-
ing around the courtyard.

Matt Trakker pointed a finger through the wind-
shield.

'*That's* what sent them packing.'

'Wow!' exclaimed Scott. 'Dragons!'

'Now we're really cooked!' whimpered T-Bob.

The guardians of the temple ambled towards them.

'They're not really dragons,' said Matt.

'Then what are they, Dad?'

'Monitor lizards. Nearest thing we've got to dragons.'

'Near enough for me!' complained T-Bob.

'They're *huge*!' said Scott.

'Yes,' noted Matt. 'What's worse is that they look very angry. VENOM obviously upset them by trying to plunder their temple. These monitor lizards want to get their own back.'

The creatures closed in on the MASK vehicles. Brad Turner brought Condor down from the sky and hovered about three metres off the ground. He was directly in the path of their advance.

'My laser cannons will scare off those lousy lizards!'

But he never got the chance to prove it.

A bolt of green lightning shot down from above and caught his helicopter a glancing blow. Condor went into a spin and crashed to the ground. Brad Turner was thrown out of his seat and his mask came off. He was not hurt but he was totally without protection.

The monitor lizards moved menacingly towards him.

He sat up and shook his head.

'What happened . . . ?'

Coming out of his daze, he saw the snarling lizards.

'Oh no!'

But his colleagues rallied around in his hour of need. Julio Lopez took immediate action inside Firefly.

'Streamer will help you to give them the slip, Brad!'

He aimed his mask and gave the command.

'Streamer oil slick – ON!'

Just as the lizards were about to reach the fallen agent, a stream of oil hit the ground and surrounded the creatures. They lost their balance and slithered all over the place. It was like watching inexperienced skaters having their first go on the ice.

Gloria Baker now lent her aid to her colleague.

'All they need now is a good, solid push.'

She aimed her mask and issued the relevant order.

'Aura – ON!'

A solid ray of energy shot out of her mask and hit the lizards. As the ray intensified, they were pushed backwards on the oil slick. Julio kept up a steady supply of oil so that the creatures continued to slither.

Shark and Firefly worked together to push the lizards across the courtyard and back into the hole from which they came. Frightened by it all, the creatures were only too glad to take refuge in the safety of their underground lair. They had met their match in the two MASK vehicles.

Matt Trakker watched it all with admiration.

'Looks like those monitor lizards have returned to their home-sweet-hole-in-the-ground!'

Scott was fascinated by the way it had been done.

'Shark and Firefly were terrific, Dad!'

'All MASK agents are trained for these emergencies.'

'Well, I'm not!' bleated T-Bob. 'I've seen enough

monsters for one day. I just want to get out of here.'

'But the lizards have gone now,' argued Scott.

The robot was not convinced the danger was over. 'They might come back out of that pit again!'

'They won't get the opportunity,' promised Matt.

He knew that his agents never left a job until it had been completed. Gloria Baker knew instinctively what to do.

'Now to put the lid on them!' she declared.

She aimed her Aura mask at the jade dragon head which was still lying on the ground where Scorpion had dropped it. The surge of energy caused the dragon head to slide back over the hole until it was sealed again.

The cork had been put back into the bottle.

Inside Thunder Hawk, Matt Trakker's mask was automatically lifted from his head. He spoke into his intercom.

'Good work!' he congratulated.

'Yeah!' added Brad, getting up and dusting himself off. 'Thanks a lot. You saved my bacon!'

Brad went quickly across to Condor to assess the damage to his vehicle. It was not extensive. The lightning bolt had dented it slightly and the crash had added further dents. But it was still operational. When he had made some running repairs, it would be as good as new.

Matt, Scott and T-Bob got out of Thunder Hawk.

'I don't know who was more scared,' observed Matt with a smile. 'VENOM or the monitor lizards.'

'*I* was more scared!' confessed T-Bob.

'There's nothing to be frightened of now,' insisted Scott.

'I hope not,' replied the robot.

'Let's take a closer look at that dragon head.'

'Okay . . . but not *too* close.'

Scott and T-Bob went across the courtyard to study the carved dragon head that was now back in place. Its eyes were still gleaming and it looked more fierce than ever.

As they hurried towards it, they forgot all about the oil slick that had been spread on the ground. Suddenly, they both lost their balance and began to skid all over the place.

'Help!' yelled T-Bob. 'I can't ice skate!'

'Hold on!' urged Scott.

Their momentum carried them on past the dragon head towards another hole in the ground. Before they could stop themselves, they dropped into the second pit.

They were dazed for a second then they heard something.

'Hiiiiiiiiisssssss!'

'Did you say "hiss", Scott?' asked T-Bob.

'No,' answered the boy nervously.

'Then who did?'

'HISS!!!'

'*He* did,' said Scott.

He pointed at the monitor lizard which had just stood up in the gloom on the other side of the pit. It

was bigger than all the others and its huge teeth were razor-sharp.

'Yow!' cried T-Bob.

'Whoah!' yelled Scott.

'This is one of those days when everything seems to go wrong!' said the robot, backing against the wall. 'Can't we give it something to calm it down, Scott. What do giant lizards eat?'

'*Us*!'

Hearing their cries, Matt rushed to the edge of the pit.

'Scott! T-Bob!'

The lizard moved in threateningly towards them.

'Why don't you pick on something your own size?' howled T-Bob at the monster. 'Like a bulldozer!'

The lizard opened its enormous jaws as wide as it could. Scott and T-Bob were within seconds of being gobbled up. There was no time for Matt to run and get his mask or for the other agents to use their high technology weapons against the creature.

It seemed as if the two of them were doomed.

Then a rescuer came sailing down into the pit.

It was Simbala.

She carried a log in her hand. As the lizard's jaws tried to snap shut, Simbala wedged the log in them. She then scooped up Scott and T-Bob before swinging back out of the pit.

'Thanks, Simbala!' said Scott.

'Yeah!' agreed T-Bob. 'Thanks "mom"!'

Simbala patted Scott on the shoulder then she gave

the robot a gentle kiss on the head. The two of them had offered her friendship when she was sad and lonely. The orang-utan had now repaid their kindness by saving their lives.

But she did not stay any longer.

Loping quickly off across the courtyard, she stopped to pick up a tiny orang-utan who was waiting for her. She cradled him in her arms and rocked him gently to and fro.

'Simbala has found her baby!' said Scott.

'That's a relief!' added T-Bob.

The orang-utan was kissing its child lovingly.

'Isn't that cute?' said Scott. 'Look at them. They act like they're almost human.'

'Yeah,' said T-Bob. 'Just like *me*!'

Laughter rang out around the courtyard.

VENOM had been put to flight once more.

Thanks to MASK, there was another happy ending.

If you have enjoyed Dragonfire, you might like to read some other MASK titles from Knight Books:

MASK 1 – THE DEATHSTONE

A meteor, which in the right hands can be the key
to a life-saving technique for mankind, but which
in the wrong hands can prove a lethal enemy, falls
to earth in the rocky desert. When VENOM come
by it, and plan to sell pieces of it off as powerful
weapons, MASK has a vital mission before it.

MASK 3 – VENICE MENACE

VENOM leader Miles Mayhem's evil scheme to
dominate the world, has brought Venice – the city
of canals – to a mysterious halt. But MASK is close
at hand.

MASK 4 – BOOK OF POWER

The revered Book of Power, holder of mystical and
ancient secrets, is sought by VENOM's leader,
Miles Mayhem, whose wicked intention is to turn
its power to his own ends.

KNIGHT BOOKS

MASK 2 – PERIL UNDER PARIS

Why does VENOM – THE VICIOUS EVIL NETWORK
OF MAYHEM, have a hideout in Paris? Are they
plotting to steal the paintings from the Louvre, or
have they a far more terrible, even deadly,
purpose?

When MASK discovers that VENOM holds a map
of Paris' underground sewage system with some
very strange locations marked onto it, they soon
realise that a terrible danger threatens the city.

The MASK mission: to save Paris from VENOM's
appalling evil. Matt Trakker, Buddie Hawkes, Scott
and T-Bob are the MASK agents dedicated to
foiling the plot before it is too late.

KNIGHT BOOKS

MASK 5 – PANDA POWER

When all the Chinese pandas are stolen from the nature preserves and a celebrated sculptor is kidnapped, MASK is not long in finding out who lies behind the crime. MASK's mission: to rescue the kidnapped from VENOM's wicked grasp.

MASK 6 – THE PLUNDER OF GLOW-WORM GROTTO

VENOM's leader, Miles Mayhem has hatched a chilling plot to steal the sacred pearls, the precious Maori heirlooms, from their secret grotto. Scott Trakker and his robot companion T-Bob help MASK in a perilous situation.

KNIGHT BOOKS

MASK 7 – THE EVERGLADES ODDITY

When Matt Trakker is laid low, Scott and his robot
T-Bob lend a hand in a dangerous assignment: to
rescue a Space Shuttle from the clutches of
VENOM.

KNIGHT BOOKS

Eight stunning MASK adventures from Knight Books

All these books are available at your local bookshop or newsagent, or can be ordered direct from the publisher. Just tick the titles you want and fill in the form below.

Prices and availability subject to change without notice.

Knight Books, P.O. Box 11, Falmouth TR10 9EN, Cornwall.

Please send cheque or postal order, and allow the following for postage and packing:

U.K. – 55p for one book, plus 22p for the second book, and 14p for each additional book ordered up to a £1.75 maximum.

B.F.P.O. and EIRE – 55p for the first book, plus 22p for the second book, and 14p per copy for the next 7 books, 8p per book thereafter.

OTHER OVERSEAS CUSTOMERS – £1.00 for the first book, plus 25p per copy for each additional book.

Please send cheque or postal order (no currency).

Name ....

Address ....

....

KNIGHT BOOKS